Help A Hamster

With grateful thanks for advice received
from the families of adopted children and our professional
experts especially Liza Bingley Miller, Independent Chair,
North Yorkshire County Council's Adoption Panel.

HR & MS

Olivia

Words by Hilary Robinson

www.hilaryrobinson.co.uk

Pictures by Mandy Stanley

www.mandystanley.com

STRAUSS HOUSE PRODUCTIONS

Lumby Grange, Lumby, South Milford, North Yorkshire, LS25 5JA

www.thecoppertree.org

First published in Great Britain 2013

Text copyright © Hilary Robinson 2013

Illustrations copyright © Mandy Stanley 2013

Hilary Robinson and Mandy Stanley have asserted their rights
to be identified as the author and illustrator of this work under
The Copyright, Designs and Patents Act, 1988

British Library Cataloguing in Publication Data

A catalogue record for this book is available from the British Library

All rights reserved. ISBN 978-0-9571245-2-3

Printed in the UK

Help A Hamster

For Lauren, Jamie, Lynda, Leah, Morgan, Joshua, Chelsey
Blake, Jayden and Daisy

Hilary Robinson & Mandy Stanley

STRAUSS HOUSE
PRODUCTIONS

My friend, Alfie Tate, is now the hamster monitor.
Mr Davis asked him to be the hamster monitor when Erika
brought our class hamster, Henry, back to school after the holidays.

Henry had given birth to four baby hamsters! We were surprised because we all thought Henry was a boy hamster.

Erika has lots of hamsters at her house.
They play and run around in the hall because Erika's mum
says that, 'even hamsters need to stretch their legs.'

Mr Davis said, 'it sounds as if hamsters have a lot of
fun at Erika's house.'

One of the baby hamsters looked small and sad.

Mr Davis said that 'a family of hamsters is called a litter.' This was 'not to be confused with the litter that we put in bins.' Alfie Tate said that a lot of geese is called a 'gaggle of geese' which we thought was funny.

I thought Henry was finding it hard to look after them all so I asked Mr Davis if we should find new homes for the baby hamsters. Mr Davis said, 'I was having exactly the same thoughts, Olivia.'

Alfie has called the sad hamster 'Alfonzo'
but the other three don't have names yet.

Alfie Tate said that he wanted to help find new homes for the hamsters because he was adopted when he was three so he knows what it's like to go and live in a new home.

Mr Davis said, 'okay Alfie,
have a chat with your mum and
dad and see what they think.'

Alfie's mum came to see the hamsters and Alfie brought a book
with him. He called it his life story book. It was given to Alfie
by the people who cared for him before he was adopted.

Alfie's STORY

Nurse Catherine

Your birth mother saw you in hospital.

Baby Alfie

My first photo

You were born on: 22nd March

At: Norwich General Hospital

You arrived between 10:20 & 10:25

Your Birth Mum

Your favourite toy...

BIRDY

It had pictures of him as a baby, his birth mum and letters from the people that helped to look after him before he came to live with his new family.

One letter from Alfie's birth mum said she really loved him but she found it difficult being a mummy.

We all wanted to help Alfie find new homes for the hamsters.

Alfie drew a picture of hamster bunk beds with a ladder so that a hamster could sleep on the top bunk if it wanted.

Barnie thought someone at his swimming club might like to adopt a hamster.

Then I went with Alfie and his mum to
put up the posters in the library...

in the corner shop, newsagent...

and at the swimming pool where Barnie goes. We sat
with his big brother Max and we watched Barnie swim.

Every day I helped Alfie clean out the hamster home and we gave them fresh food and water.

Alfonzo still seemed a bit sad and got pushed away
from the bowl by the others so we fed him ourselves.

Alfie said he didn't know hamsters could
be bullies like people could be sometimes.

He said when people rang up he asked them lots of hamstery questions like, 'what would you do if a hamster had a tummy ache?'

Then our head teacher, Mr Banks, Alfie's mum and Alfie decided which hamster would be happy in which home. But Mr Banks thought Alfonzo still needed some special care from us.

Henry still didn't seem to be able to care for Alfonzo.

Alfie drew a picture of a hamster with a sad face. Alfie says he can't remember if he had a sad face. He said he couldn't remember if he was sad before he was adopted but he thinks he might have been.

Alfie's mum came to school. She had chatted with Alfie, Alfie's dad and his brothers and sisters. She asked Mr Banks and Mr Davis if they could adopt Alfonzo!

So now Alfonzo has a new family.

Alfie says Alfonzo likes his new home because he has his own hamster bowl, he can run around and everyone loves him.

Then guess what Alfie made for Alfonzo? He made him...

Olivia

Photograph by Mandy's niece

Esme

Photograph by www.marjoleinleusink.nl

Marjolein

Alfie →

STRAUSS HOUSE
PRODUCTIONS

Blue Barn Farm

Book four in the Copper Tree Series

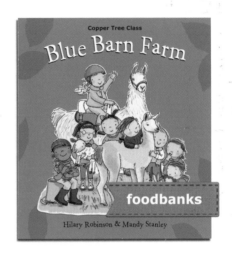

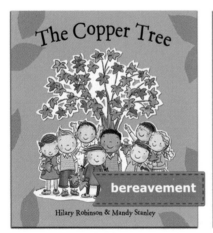

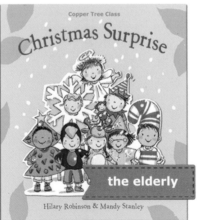

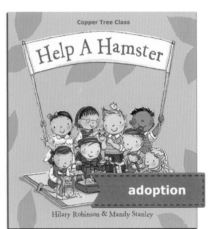

Helping Children to Help Themselves

www.strausshouseproductions.com

www.thecoppertree.org